JOY ROBERTSON

PRINCESS AMIYAH

VOLUME 1

Auctorem House
276 5th Ave, Ste 704-2591
New York, NY 10001
www.auctoremhouse.com
1.888.332.7718

She was born Amiyah Joy in the kingdom of Nostrebor. Some called her AJ, but her grandmother called her Princess Amiyah because she recognized that she was born with a very special gift. It was the same gift that was evident in her grandfather, the Grand Duke of Nostrebor, Prince Rosford, who lost his life under dubious circumstance. It was alleged that his older brother, Prince Jaydomi, had a yearning to rule Nostrebor. When the kingdom was given to Prince Rosford, his older brother made a declaration that as the firstborn, he should have been given control of the kingdom. When they return from the annual moons of hunting, it was feared that Prince Jaydomi had done something unthinkable to his brother, but it could not be proven. Prince Rosford laid ill in the kingdom for quite some time until he succumbs to his illness. The inevitable happened, and Prince Jaydomi had indeed gained control of Nostrebor, and the family of Prince Rosford was relegated to an inferior part of the kingdom of Nostrebor.©

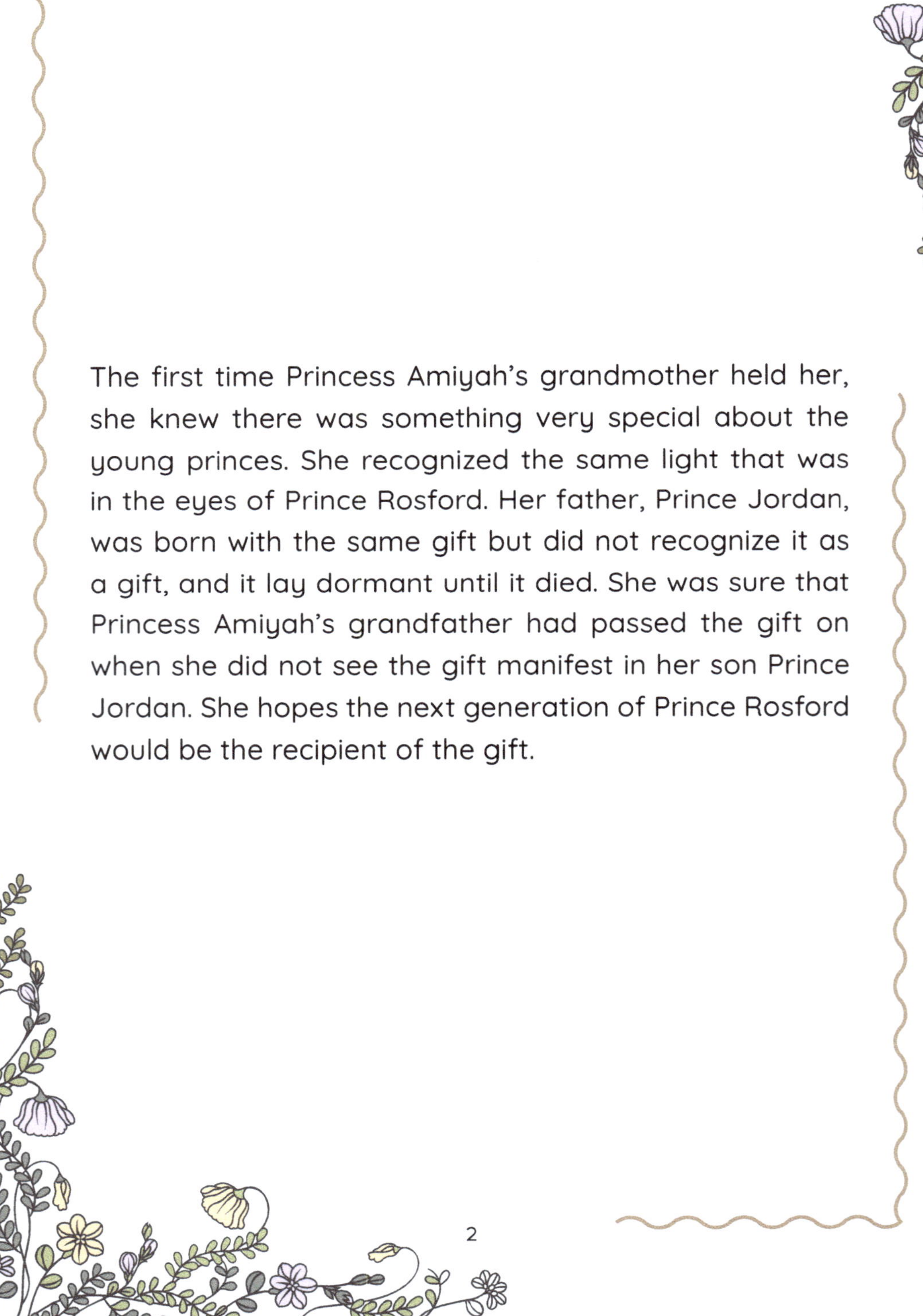

The first time Princess Amiyah's grandmother held her, she knew there was something very special about the young princes. She recognized the same light that was in the eyes of Prince Rosford. Her father, Prince Jordan, was born with the same gift but did not recognize it as a gift, and it lay dormant until it died. She was sure that Princess Amiyah's grandfather had passed the gift on when she did not see the gift manifest in her son Prince Jordan. She hopes the next generation of Prince Rosford would be the recipient of the gift.

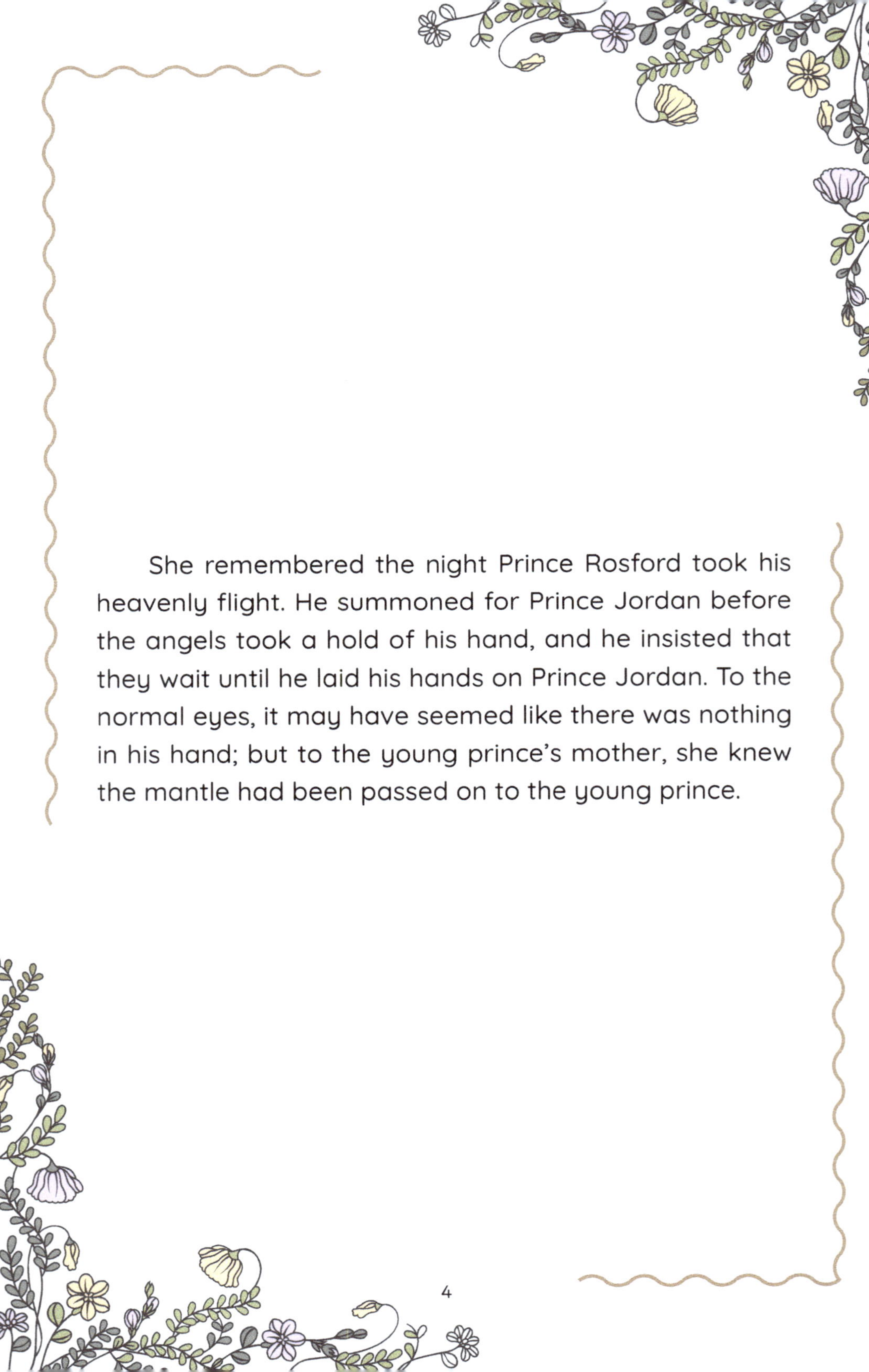

She remembered the night Prince Rosford took his heavenly flight. He summoned for Prince Jordan before the angels took a hold of his hand, and he insisted that they wait until he laid his hands on Prince Jordan. To the normal eyes, it may have seemed like there was nothing in his hand; but to the young prince's mother, she knew the mantle had been passed on to the young prince.

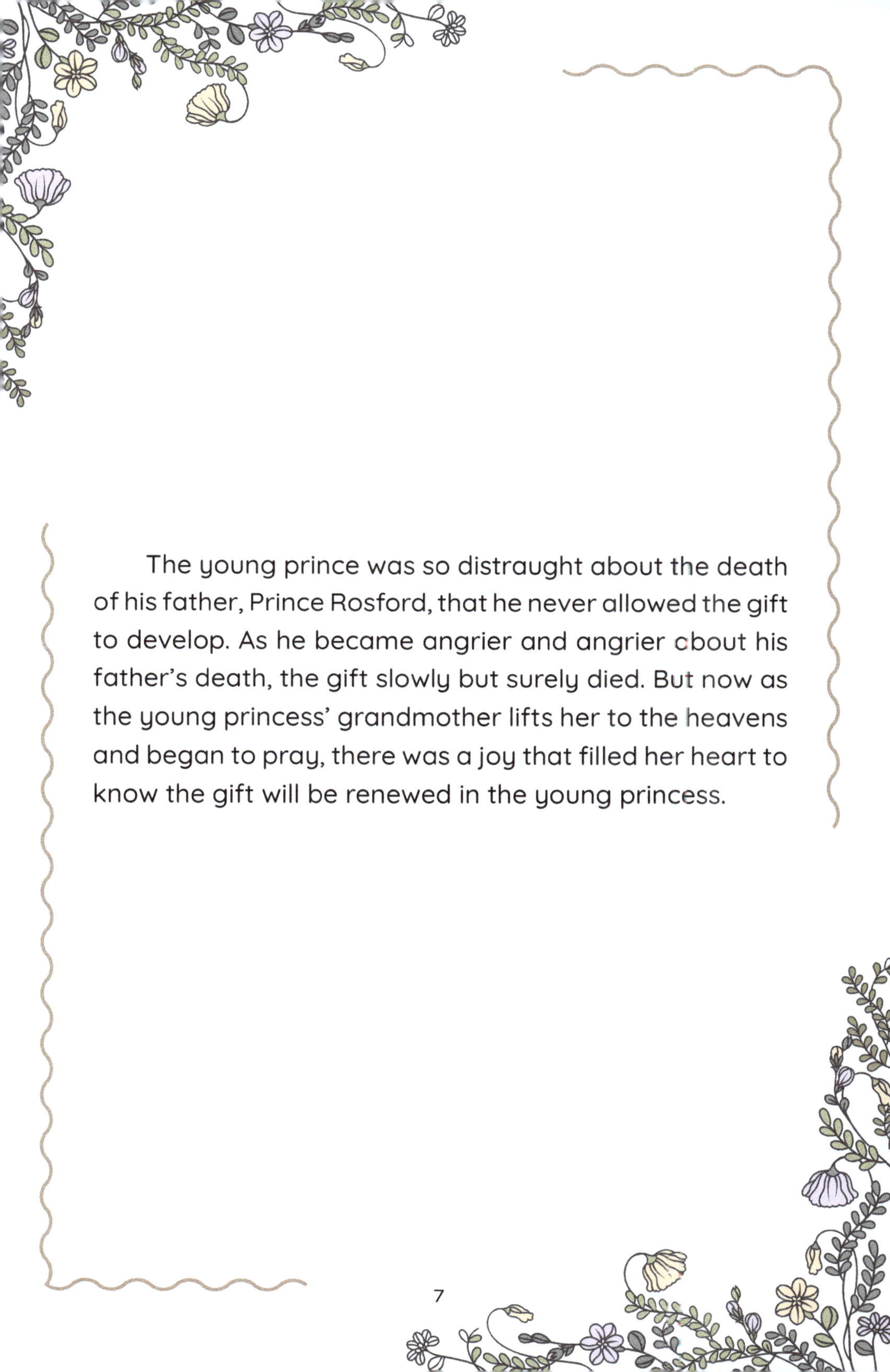

The young prince was so distraught about the death of his father, Prince Rosford, that he never allowed the gift to develop. As he became angrier and angrier about his father's death, the gift slowly but surely died. But now as the young princess' grandmother lifts her to the heavens and began to pray, there was a joy that filled her heart to know the gift will be renewed in the young princess.

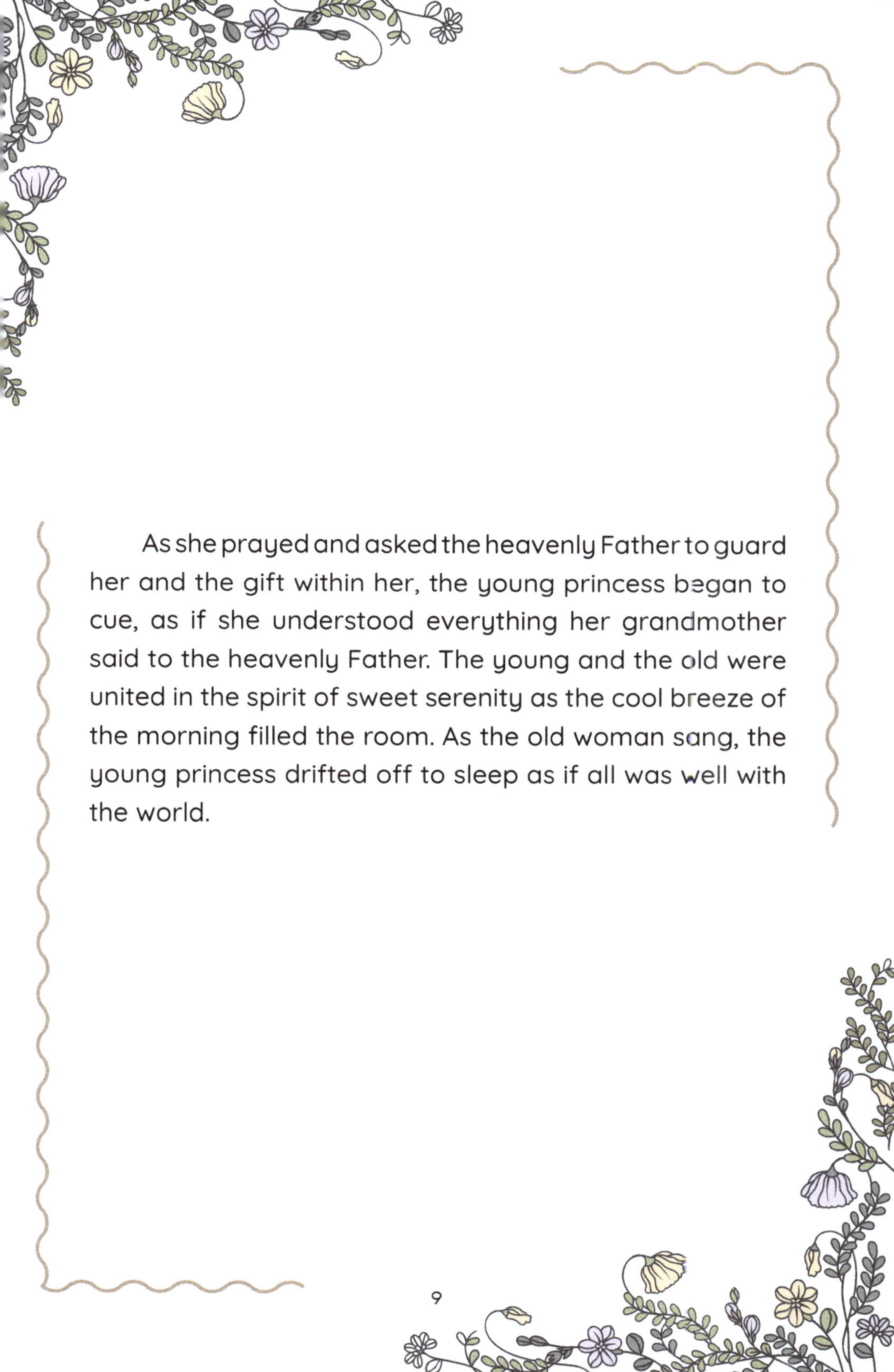

As she prayed and asked the heavenly Father to guard her and the gift within her, the young princess began to cue, as if she understood everything her grandmother said to the heavenly Father. The young and the old were united in the spirit of sweet serenity as the cool breeze of the morning filled the room. As the old woman sang, the young princess drifted off to sleep as if all was well with the world.

As the young princess began to grow, she grew more and more beautiful with each year that pass, and the wisdom she gained was beyond her young years although her family was relegated to a lesser part of the kingdom. Everyone who came into Nostrebor who had a desire to see the young princess realized there was something supernatural about Princess Amiyah. They were never the same when they left the presence of the young princess. The word began to spread in the kingdom of Nostrebor as the young princess grew; it was clear by her kindness to others that she was very special, unlike any other child who was born in the kingdom.

An instant joy filled the hearts of anyone who came into her presence. It was hard for anyone to explain what they were feeling when they touch the young princess, except that there was an instant comfort that came over them as if someone had covered them with a warm blanket. The face of the young princess glows each time she smiles. She gave off the radiant effect of the warm morning sun. What was it that made everyone gravitate to the young princess? Surely! It was more than the little princess beauty. It was the gift that the heavenly Father had bestowed upon her that she through His love would draw the world to Him. The young princess had a great influence on others in the kingdom of Nostrebor, and that made Prince Jaydomi quite angry each time someone requested to see the young princes.

He was convinced that by banishing Prince Rosford's family to the lesser-known part of the kingdom, the interest in the young princess would subside, but her fame grew; and through her gift from the heavenly Father, she was able to explain how they could be pardoned for the wrong they had done because the Father loved them with an absolute love called agape.

Her brother, Prince Camry, was extremely happy when he heard that the heavenly Father could pardon him because he had disobeyed his mother and father and had broken a very costly family heirloom when he was told it was not a toy and he should not touch it, but he allowed his curiosity to get the best of him, and the heirloom that had been in the kingdom of Nostrebor for four generations was broken into a million pieces.

Prince Camryn was so excited about the pardon that he ran all the way to the adjoining kingdom of Drofsor to tell his cousin, Prince Trae, that the heavenly Father had pardoned him for disobeying his mother and father and for breaking the family heirloom. Prince Trae asked Prince Camryn, "How do you know this?"

"Princess Amiyah told me."

"And you believe her?"

"The light in her eyes made me believe."

Prince Trae wanted to believe, but he had his doubts. He must see the princess for himself. If this was true, he too could be pardoned. He was quite mean to his cousin Prince Malachi, who was visiting from the Kingdom of Nadroj. He did not want his cousin to visit because he commanded too much attention. Whenever Prince Malachi visited, everyone would gather around him to hear the many languages that he spoke. That made Prince Trae quite angry. He hated prince Malachi, but if the heavenly Father could pardon him, he was sure his attitude toward prince Malachi would change, and he would feel so much better inside.

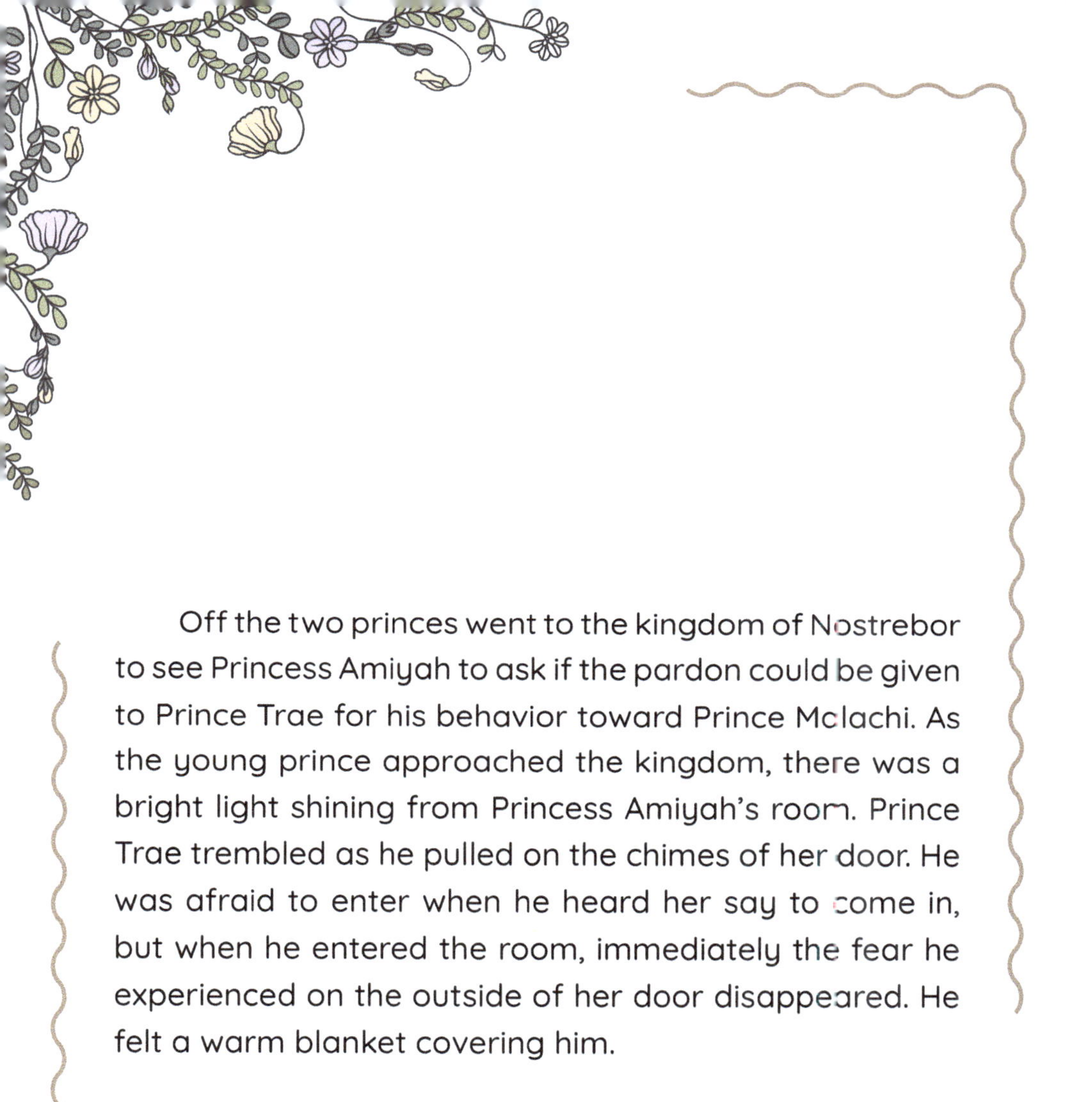

Off the two princes went to the kingdom of Nostrebor to see Princess Amiyah to ask if the pardon could be given to Prince Trae for his behavior toward Prince Mclachi. As the young prince approached the kingdom, there was a bright light shining from Princess Amiyah's room. Prince Trae trembled as he pulled on the chimes of her door. He was afraid to enter when he heard her say to come in, but when he entered the room, immediately the fear he experienced on the outside of her door disappeared. He felt a warm blanket covering him.

His lips trembled as he asked Princess Amiyah, "Will the heavenly Father pardon me for my behavior toward Prince Malachi as he did for Prince Camryn?"

The young princess smiled as she took the hands of Prince Trae. "Prince Trae," she said softly, "the heavenly Father loves you equally as He loves Prince Camryn, and He can pardon you with the same agape parcon that He has given to Prince Camryn, and you simply must believe that!"

"I do," he said softly. "I feel the light of the Father manifesting in me, and I must bear witness to the light that my joy may be filled." Prince Trae thanked the Princess for the gift of light he received.

He scoured off to find his cousin Prince Malachi and tell him about the wonderful news he had received. Through the castle, he dashed knocking over Prince Malachi, who was approaching the gate.

"Trae! You did that on purpose!" the prince cried.

"No, I didn't, Malachi. I was coming to tell you about the agape pardon I received from the heavenly Father and how it made me feel different inside and to let you know I no longer have envy in my heart toward you because the Father has granted me the language of truth, which now abides in me. I hope that you will grant me your pardon as well, Malachi."

Prince Malachi was astonished at the change in Trae. He had always known that Trae resented him, but now, there was a real change in him. "Can anyone receive this agape pardon?" asked Malachi.

"Why, Malachi! Do you need this agape pardon as well? I have always thought you were perfect!"

"Perfect! No, not perfect. I have grief in my heart toward the new baby that is coming because I will not be the center of attention when my baby brother comes. I have not told this to anyone, but when Mother and Father announced we were going to have a new addition to the family, I was less than pleased because I knew the new baby would take up so much of Mother and Father's time."

"Well, come with us, and we will take you to Princess Amiyah, and she will show you how the heavenly Father can grant you the same agape pardon that has been given to Camryn and me."

The three princes went off to see the young princess. As they approached the kingdom of Nostrebor, they could see the radiant light from the princess' window. Trae assured Malachi he should not be afraid of the light. It was the light from the heavenly Father that lights the princess wherever she was, and it was that light that led him to the knowledge of the truth rather than the spirit of error.

The three entered the princess' room. There was no need to tell her why they were there again. She simply took Prince Malachi's hand and asked if he believe the heavenly Father loves him as he loves Prince Camryn and Prince Trae.

Prince Malachi nodded his head gently and asked, "Can the heavenly Father help me to love my new baby brother as well when he comes?"

"Malachi, the heavenly Father will not only help you love the new baby. He will also cause you to love everyone from this day on. Seeing others through the eyes of the heavenly Father will cause you to love others as the heavenly Father has loved you. For this is the message that we have heard from the beginning that we should love one another as the heavenly Father has loved us."

The three princes left the young princess, with a clear assurance that they were loved and pardoned by the heavenly Father.

ABOUT THE AUTHOR

Joy Robertson is a speaker and author who migrated from Montreal, Canada, in the early nineties. She is a resident of San Antonio, Texas. Her first book, Broken Covenant (A Family in Crisis), is a telling and raw story about conquering the devastation of death and loss. It leaves you with a sense of hope when everything around you says it's hopeless. It is truly a testament to God's love and grace. It has been featured on the radio program Unshackled in dramatic form and is being heard in one hundred and fifty-seven countries and fifty-four different languages.

Her second book Princess Amiyah Volume 1 is a new series of children's books that she hopes will give young readers and their parents another option for bedtimes stories from a biblical perspective. She is a mother of four and grandmother of five.